love 'em or liam

dog tags
book four

Kat Baxter

Adorkable Hot Mess Press

Love 'em or Liam

Kat Baxter

Edited by: Emily Beierle-McKaskle

Copyeditor: BookReadingJenn and Geeky Girl Author Services

Book cover: Cormar Covers

Cover image: CJC Photography

Cover model: Eric Guilmette

Formatted with Vellum

love 'em or liam

WREN

I never thought I'd marry again, especially since my first was an epic failure. But a threat to my son's custody has me making a call to the one man I trust, Liam Gregory. My first crush. My best friend. Off-limits in every way. Liam readily agrees to be my husband… but this isn't just paperwork to him. Not when he looks at me like that. And definitely not when he touches me like I already belong to him.

LIAM

I left town after high school and joined the ARMY because I knew Wren Ashcroft deserved better than the likes of me. Then she married my best friend. Now widowed and emotionally bruised from their sham of a marriage she needs my help. I'll protect her. I'll marry her. But I'm done holding back how I feel. She's my wife now—and I'll make damn sure she knows exactly what that means.

chapter **one**

WREN

It's moments like these when I wish my husband had been better. A better husband. A better father. Hell, just a better human.

But he hadn't been, and it made playing the part of the grieving widow really damn hard sometimes.

Frankly, it was just exhausting—all the pretending. Pretending I'd ever loved him. Pretending he'd ever loved me. Pretending he hadn't died with too much OxyContin in his body at a seedy hotel with his latest flavor of the week. Her name had been Sheila.

I suppose I should thank my in-laws for their

ability to clean up their son's messes, no matter how big or scandalous. At least most of the good people of Big Wood, Tennessee, didn't know the depth of my embarrassment and shame. Or how far the golden boy had fallen.

Colt and I were a mistake from the moment we ended up in bed together. We'd been using each other as a substitute for the man who'd left us both. Our mutual best friend, Liam Gregory. Liam had been the glue that held together our little trio of friends, right up until he'd joined the army right after high school graduation.

I'd missed him so damn much. We both had.

One night, Colt and I were reminiscing, and one thing led to another, which led to naked times. We both agreed the next day that it had been a mistake and we would just move on. But then I'd found out I was pregnant.

His parents had demanded that we marry immediately. I'd been lonely and scared of raising a baby on my own, so I'd agreed. Colt had been great that first year, during my pregnancy, and shortly after Keller was born. Then everything had changed.

Colt had wrecked his motorcycle. The chronic

pain changed his personality. Then the addiction to the pain killers started. In truth, I still don't know if the affairs happened before or after that. I do know that the last three years of our marriage—before Colt OD'd—we hadn't shared a bed. Once I knew he was sleeping with other women, I was done.

So yeah, we had a decent marriage for a year and then everything went to shit. There was no getting a divorce, though, because his parents were further into our marriage than Colt ever was. We lived in a house they bought and furnished. They had their fingers in every aspect of my life.

"You don't need to work. Good mothers stay home with their children, even after they start school."

"If you divorce Colten, you will end up on the wrong side of everything, Wren. You don't want that kind of damage done to your reputation."

Now those meddling jerks are after my son. I sought some legal advice from a lawyer who lives in a different state. There was no way I could ask someone in Big Wood or even Knoxville because if the Bishops got wind of me looking to fight them, they'd make everything harder on me. As it is, they likely think I'm just going to hand Keller over to them.

I've been playing nice with them for the last eight years and I am done. They will not get their hands on my son. Which is why I'm currently holding my phone and trying to decide if this is a phone call question or if I need to video chat with the one man I trust to help me figure this situation out. Liam Gregory.

My phone pings with an incoming message and I nearly drop the device. But it's a text from my sister.

WINNIE: Have you called him yet?

ME: No.

WINNIE: Want me to?

ME: *snort. I don't think that's how this should go. But thanks for the offer.

WINNIE: Just rip off the bandage, Wren. This is Liam we're talking about. He would do anything for you.

ME: Maybe once upon a time he would. But I haven't seen him in years.

ME: And this is a huge favor that will completely upend his life.

WINNIE: Do you have other options?

ME: None that I can think of. Unless I want to change our names and move out of the country. But with their financial resources, they'd find me eventually.

WINNIE: Assholes.

ME: Yep.

ME: So how goes the job hunting?

WINNIE: I've put in applications at all of the elementary schools and preschools in the surrounding area. But nothing yet.

WINNIE: Oh, and I signed up for a nanny matching service.

ME: Great idea. Maybe one of the wealthy families will hire you, and you can spend the summer playing with cute kids by a backyard pool.

WINNIE: If only.

WINNIE: CALL HIM!

ME: Okay. I'm doing it right now. Promise.

WINNIE: If you don't, I'm coming over there and calling for you.

I blow out a breath. She's right. Yes, this is a big ask, but also, my kid is on the line. I refuse to let my manipulative in-laws raise my son. They did a shitty job raising their own. I can't let them destroy Keller.

Before I can talk myself out of it, I find Liam's contact in my phone and tap the phone icon. It starts ringing, and my whole chest feels like it's filled with carbonation.

"Hey Songbird," Liam's husky baritone voice comes over the line.

"Hi. Liam. Hello." Wow, I'm off to a great

start. Maybe I can tell him this is the first time I've ever made a phone call. Which he obviously would know was a lie because we've spent hours on the phone together over the course of the last fifteen years.

He chuckles. "How are you?"

"I'm good. And you?"

"God, it's good to hear your voice." There's the sound of fabric rustling and I'm guessing he's lying in bed.

"Thanks."

"What's going on, Wren? I can tell something is wrong."

I release a shaky breath. "I need a favor."

"Anything," he says immediately.

"No, don't answer yet. Because this isn't like, hey can you let me borrow your car or something. It's much bigger. And I hate that this is why I'm calling for the first time in months."

"Don't do that," he says.

"What?"

"Act like we're acquaintances without history. What have I always told you?"

My heart is pounding so loudly, it feels like my ears are vibrating. "That we'll always be best friends. No matter what."

"Exactly. Now ask your favor, but just know that the answer is already yes. Because I would do anything for you, Wren. You know that."

Why is he so perfect? Why didn't I tell him before he left for the Army how I felt about him? Maybe we could've been together this entire time. And he would be Keller's father. Not a spoiled, only child whose parents indulged his every desire.

"Colt's parents are filing for full custody of Keller," I say.

"What? Why the fuck would they do that?"

"To punish me? Honestly, I don't know. They rarely spend time with him. Just buy him fancy toys and bring him to their country club wearing the most ridiculous little blazer."

Liam chuffs out a laugh. "Colt had one of those."

"I guess maybe they see this as another chance since raising Colt was obviously a failure."

"What can I do to help? Do you need money?"

Oh, if only it were that easy. For the hundredth time, I mentally hated that I have to ask him this. I take a quick breath, then just blurted it out.

"I need a husband."

Silence ticks by with the seconds on the microwave clock.

I close my eyes. He's going to say no. Shit.

"Liam?"

"I'm here, Songbird, just trying to understand precisely what you're asking me."

"I'm asking you to marry me. The lawyer I spoke to said that they wouldn't have a leg to stand on in this custody case if I were married. One of their main reasons is me being a single mother. So being in a committed relationship would go a long way in proving to a judge that Keller should stay with me."

"They probably have every judge in three counties in their pockets," Liam says.

"They've certainly said as much to me."

Liam is silent for a few breaths. I try to think of something to say to let him off the hook, but nothing comes to mind.

"I will take care of everything. I'll send you the plans via email," he says.

"What does that mean exactly?"

"It means that I'll meet you in Vegas so we can tie the knot. Then I'll come back home with you and pack you and Keller up to move you to Texas with me. That okay?"

Relief washes over me so fully and completely, I nearly sink to the floor. "Yes. I will miss Winnie fiercely, but getting out of the Bishops' orbit would be life-changing."

"Then it's settled. I'll take care of everything. Leave Keller with Winnie and let's go get hitched?"

"Are you sure, Liam? This is such a huge, life-changing thing. I mean, we can stay out of your hair as much as possible, and I'll try to find a job to cover our costs because I don't want to be a financial burden."

"Wren, stop talking about shit like that. I've got you, baby. Let me take care of you."

He has no idea what those words do to me. I can't really remember anyone ever taking care of me. Mine and Winnie's parents were distant, to say the least. As the oldest kid, it was up to me to take care of my sister. Then I had Keller. Then there was Colt.

But to have someone take care of me? That seems like a dream far out of reach.

chapter **two**

LIAM

I hang up the phone and immediately get to work on booking plane tickets for both of us as well as a hotel room. I do some preliminary research on chapels and mark down a few to make inquiries about.

My phone pings on the desk next to me, and I see it's the group chat from my buddies. At one point, we were all in the same unit for ARMY Rangers, but now we're civilians running a dog sanctuary together.

EVAN: Did I miss it? I'm gonna be pissed if I missed it.

ME: Miss what?

EVAN: Beau's ass kicking.

BEAU: Ass kicking?

BEAU: What are you talking about?

BEAU: Flynn is here with me now. He's the big spoon to my little spoon.

FLYNN: For fuck's sake.

These guys are fucking nuts. But I love them. I am glad to know that Flynn didn't kill Beau for hooking up with Flynn's younger sister.

Beau's always been the wildest one in our group. He was the grenadier though, and that's kind of what you need to have someone go into unknown situations and blow shit up. But seeing him with Daisy, watching him fall in love with a woman pregnant with another man's baby, has been pretty fucking cool.

FLYNN: For the record, I am spooning my wife.

EVAN: So there was no ass kicking?

EVAN: Y'all suck.

ROMEO: I'll kick your ass, Evan, if you really need me to.

ME: Now, that I would watch.

JACK: Why must we have these group chats at all hours of the day?

DANE: Because they don't have warm, willing women to spend their time with.

FLYNN: Some of us do.

I suppose I should tell them about what I'm about to do. Especially since I'll be away from work for a few days. Right now we all have unofficial jobs at the sanctuary. Mine is coordinating with shelters and other non-profits to bring in new dogs that are in danger of being euthanized. Or dogs that have been in abusive and neglectful situations. But I can do most of that from anywhere.

I'll just make sure that Dane is looped into

any of my communication so he can manage things on-site.

ME: While we're all here, I'm leaving town for a few days.

ROMEO: Everything okay?

ME: I'm getting married.

EVAN: Say what, now?

BEAU: Have you been secretly dating someone?

FLYNN: Not everyone dates in secret.

BEAU: For the record, we haven't even been on an official date. We were just cohabitating.

FLYNN: That does not make me feel better.

BEAU: I plan to remedy that very soon.

EVAN: There could still be a fight.

ROMEO: Kids! Be quiet and let the adults talk. Liam, details.

ME: An old friend. Widow of an even older friend.

ME: Custody issue.

ME: We're meeting in Vegas.

ME: I'll have more details when we get back.

ROMEO: Is this a good thing?

ME: It's complicated.

ME: But it's the right thing.

EVAN: Another one bites the dust.

EVAN: That just leaves me and you, Romeo.

ROMEO: I'm not marrying you, kid.

BEAU: Good luck.

ME: Thanks.

BEAU: Daisy and I are official.

DANE: I knew you were different.

FLYNN: It's annoying that he loves her.

FLYNN: I really wanted to kick his ass.

BEAU: But I do love her. More than anything.

FLYNN: I can't kick his ass when he's being good to my sister. But if he steps out of line.

EVAN: I'll hold him down.

ROMEO: Bloodthirsty much, kid?

JACK: Seriously. Evan, you're our medic. What happened to do no harm?

EVAN: If I'm not the one harming someone, then it's fair game.

ROMEO: You need to get out more.

DANE: Just be patient. Saddle Creek has a festival about every three weeks.

BEAU: Really?

DANE: Not quite, but it feels like that sometimes.

DANE: Small towns in Texas gotta celebrate everything.

ROMEO: I'm going back to bed. See you fuckers at work later.

I send a copy of my flight information to Dane and Romeo, then send Wren hers. I'm about to silence my phone when it pings with another text. This one is outside of the group chat, though.

ROMEO: Is this that bird girl?

ME: If by 'bird girl' you mean Wren, then yes.

ROMEO: So you're finally getting what you want.

ME: That's not what this is about. She needs my help.

ROMEO: And the fact that you get to marry the girl you've loved your entire life doesn't matter?

ME: This isn't about me.

ME: Colt's parents are suing for custody of her son.

ME: Remarrying will protect her from that happening.

ROMEO: You bringing them back here to live with you?

ME: Of course. She's gonna be my fucking wife. I'm not leaving her in Tennessee.

ROMEO: Well, I look forward to meeting the woman who has had you in knots the entire time I've known you.

ME: Fuck you. Wait until you meet someone, tough guy.

ROMEO: I meet someones all the time.

ME: Fucker.

But even after I silence my phone, I'm not able to silence Romeo's voice in my head.

He's not wrong about how I feel about Wren. How I've always felt about her.

In high school, she wasn't just the girl I loved from afar. She was also one of my best friends. I would have made a play for her back then, but I didn't have shit to offer her. I knew she deserved better than what I could give her.

Somewhere in the back of my mind, I might have had a plan that involved getting my shit together and coming home a hero ready to sweep her off her feet.

Needless to say, that plan died a brutal death when I found out she was married to my other best friend, Colt.

Their marriage just about killed me, but I tried to make my peace with it. I knew he could give the kind of financial and personal stability I never could. I wanted a good life for her. And if he'd made her happy, I would have stayed away forever.

Hell, even when I got wind that he wasn't making her happy, I stayed away. It wasn't my place to interfere. Wren has always been strong and single-minded. I knew if she needed my help, she would ask for it. She never did.

Until now.

Now that she needs me, I'll move heaven and earth to do right by her.

chapter **three**

WREN

Today is my wedding day.

My second wedding day, yet somehow this one feels more real than the big church ceremony felt. I stare up at the lit neon sign hanging above the double wooden doors leading into the chapel. *Little Chapel of Love* blinks back at me in pink and blue.

Tucked just off the Strip, the little white church looks like something from a vintage postcard. It's a small, white clapboard building with a pitched pink roof and candy-striped awnings.

An instrumental love song drifts from

hidden outdoor speakers, cheerful and slightly tinny. It's definitely trying to give off romantic vibes, though the horns and traffic noises from the Strip still hang in the air.

I smooth a hand down my skirt for probably the fiftieth time. This is definitely not like the dress I wore to my first wedding. That one had been picked out by my then- future mother-in-law. I'd foolishly thought she was helping because she knew I didn't have a mother to go through all the wedding planning with me.

The signs were there from the beginning, but it took me a while longer to see the level of curation that was going on from the sidelines. So no floor-length white gown today. Nope, I'm wearing a sassy red knee-length dress that hugs my curves and then flares at the waist to a fun and frilly skirt. I've paired it with black flats because no one wants to walk in the Vegas heat in stilettos.

Liam texted me he was on the way and that he had my bouquet with him, as well as the rings. My heart feels like a horde of tap dancers has moved into my chest and is rehearsing nonstop. I try some more deep breathing, but I end up holding my breath.

Why am I so nervous?

"Hey Songbird."

Liam's voice comes from behind me, and I steel myself before I turn to face him. When I am finally face-to-face with him, I realize immediately that I am not prepared. Not even a little bit.

High school Liam was hot.

Army Liam was even hotter.

This man standing in front of me is like a whole new person. He's dressed in a suit that must be bespoke, with the way it molds to his broad shoulders and thick thighs. His brown hair frames his face in effortless waves.

He smiles and pulls me into an embrace. He's like a solid wall of muscle pressed against me, his strong arms wrapped around my body. And he smells like sin. That's the only thing I can think of. It's earthy and decadent, and I want to bury my face in the crook of his neck.

He steps back, but grabs one of my hands. His dark brown eyes trail over my frame. Heat follows in the wake of his perusal, and it's definitely from more than the Vegas temperature.

"You look gorgeous, Wren." His swallow is visible as his Adam's apple bobs. Then he holds out the bouquet of all white flowers to me.

White roses, daisies, calla lilies, and baby's-breath mixed together with only the smallest amount of greenery.

"It's beautiful. Thank you."

"My bride deserves pretty flowers," he says.

His bride. I am so in over my head with this man.

"You ready to do this?" he asks.

"Absolutely," I say with a confidence I don't feel. But I will do anything for Keller.

Liam leads me into the chapel and there's a small narthex outside of the main chapel area. There's a glass case with tiaras and rings and other things for sale. Liam walks straight the counter and speaks to the older woman standing there.

"Gregory wedding," he says.

Gregory. Wren Gregory. God, how many times did I doodle that on my school notebooks? Too many times to count. It's kind of a miracle he never caught me.

The artificial scent of vanilla permeates the air and I can see through the door into the small chapel area that there are candles lit.

"Yes, Mr. Gregory. They're ready for you now," the woman says. "Of course you have plenty of time since you reserved the chapel for the entire hour." She looks down at her clipboard, then walks around the counter. "I'll just give you two a moment. Step in through those doors when you're ready."

"Why did you reserve the chapel for so long? This doesn't need to be a big deal, Liam. I didn't want you to go to so much trouble or expense. We just need this to be legal."

He steps in closer to me, then even closer so that I'm backed up against that glass case. "I can lie to the officiant. I can lie to your in-laws. But I refuse to lie to myself."

I search his face. "Liam—"

His arms go around me, bracing on the counter behind me. "If all you want is a fake husband, you need to pick someone else. If you want me..." His intense gaze locks on my lips, then slowly raises to my eyes. "That comes with everything."

My lower belly pulls. Arousal, hot and wet, seeps into my panties. I want to ask him what he means by everything, but all I can do is nod. Because the truth is, he's the only one I trust with this.

He leans in closer and presses his lips just

below my right ear. My eyes flutter closed and my body leans into his touch. I'm so starved for affection it should be embarrassing, but I can't muster up that feeling. Probably because right now horny is driving my emotion bus.

Then he steps away.

"Let's get married," he says.

I really hope I'm not panting. Or drooling. I feel like a complete mess, but I follow his lead and step into the main chapel.

Fairy lights cover much of the ceiling, giving the small room an ethereal glow. Maybe I'm drunk on his brief touch because this tiny Vegas chapel suddenly feels like the most romantic place in the world. Even with the accents of gold cherubs and rhinestone hearts.

He takes my hand, threads our fingers together and we walk down the center aisle. Four pews line each side, the ends of the wooden benches are decorated with lace bows. Faintly in the background, I hear Pachelbel's Canon piped in on the speakers.

The officiant—an older gentleman wearing a powder-blue tuxedo—stands at the front and smiles genuinely at us.

"Welcome, you two," he says. "I'll be

marrying you today. My wife, Loretta here," he points to the woman sitting in the pew. She's the same one from the front desk area. "Will be acting as your witness."

We reach him and he holds out a sheet of paper to Liam.

"If you could double-check the names," he says.

Liam nods.

"Face each other then and hold hands," the officiant says.

Once mine and Liam's eyes meet, the man's words fade into the background.

I repeat my vows, watch Liam's mouth as he repeats his, then stare as my best friend slides a gorgeous ring onto my finger. He hands me a plain band to give to him.

"I now pronounce you husband and wife. You may kiss your bride," the officiant says.

"She was a bride," Liam says. "Now, she's my wife." Then his mouth is on mine. It's not a polite kiss. Not a wedding in a church kiss. Nope, he slants his lips across mine and slides his tongue into my mouth.

I'm hopeless to do anything but kiss him back.

chapter **four**

WREN

ME: I'm in trouble

WINNIE: What happened?

ME: Liam just kissed the hell out of me. I think I'm having an out of body experience.

WINNIE: It's about damn time. So you're married?

ME: Yes. We're on our way back to our hotel room.

ME: Right before we walked down the aisle he told me if I wanted a fake husband, I needed to marry someone else. That this would be a real marriage.

WINNIE: Sigh.

ME: I'm pretty sure he just meant sex.

WINNIE: YES!!! Ride that man like the stallion he is.

ME: Please don't ever say those words again.

WINNIE: Which ones specifically? Would you prefer: climb him like a tree? Or sit on him like your favorite chair?

ME: Stop!

WINNIE: All I'm trying to say is that you've loved this guy since you were in high school. And you trust him. He's not going to hurt you or Keller.

ME: I don't know that I still have that part of me. The ability to love like that.

ME: I mean, I loved Colt too. Or I thought I did, once upon a time. And then he broke me over and over again. I don't think I have any space left for that kind of romantic love.

WINNIE: Oh honey… Colt was a selfish man-child dickhead.

WINNIE: Liam is different on possibly every level.

ME: Maybe, but I don't think I know how to love anyone but my kid anymore.

WINNIE: You love me.

ME: True.

WINNIE: And you still love Liam. Otherwise you wouldn't have called him to marry you like this.

WINNIE: He just told you he wants a real marriage!

WINNIE: I think he's going to wear you down. Great sex has a way of working magic.

WINNIE: And Liam has always had Big Dick Energy.

ME: You are the absolute worst.

ME: And like you'd know. You've never even touched a dick.

WINNIE: But I've seen them in porn.

WINNIE: Oh, and that one time Ben Sanders flashed everybody when he streaked across the football field.

WINNIE: Course that's when everyone started calling him Tiny Ben.

WINNIE: But back to your situation. He's your husband now.

ME: Still…

WINNIE: When was the last time you had an orgasm without batteries involved?

ME: Why are you like this?

WINNIE: I require an answer.

ME: Uh… never.

WINNIE: Wait…

WINNIE: Seriously?

WINNIE: All that time with Colt?

ME: First of all, I wouldn't let him touch me the last three years of our marriage.

ME: Initially he would try, but nothing ever worked.

ME: I think I might be frigid.

ME: I faked it with Colt. Even from the beginning.

WINNIE: Why did you never tell me this before?

ME: What would have been the point?

WINNIE: All the more reason for you to consummate your marriage.

ME: Well, it won't be happening tonight.

ME: Also, I still haven't told him y'all are in the hotel suite.

chapter five

LIAM

Sitting in the back of the limo as we ride to our hotel, all I can think is that Wren is finally mine. I'm going to blame my special forces training for the fact that I managed to read that entire text exchange between Wren and her sister. I wasn't trying to eavesdrop, per se, but then I saw the word orgasm, my curiosity was piqued.

I'm pissed off at Colt all over again. He had Wren for years and he never made her come. What a selfish fucker.

Figuratively and literally.

I force myself to turn away from her phone

and stare instead at the bright & colorful lights of the Vegas strip.

Finally we reach the hotel and a doorman opens my door. I reach in to help Wren out.

She looks so goddamn beautiful in that dress. The red curve- hugging top makes her tits look amazing. It won't be happening tonight but I definitely want to fuck those beauties.

The bells and flashing lights surround us as we skim the outside of the casino floor until I find a straight shot through a bank of quarter slot machines. Finally we reach the elevators that will lead us up to our suite. I booked a suite. Despite the fact that I would love to go upstairs and do at least three of the filthy things I've wanted to do to her since I was seventeen, she clearly needs more time. She seemed legitimately surprised that I mean for our marriage to be real. She might need time getting used to the idea of us sleeping together.

Not to mention that orgasm bomb she dropped on her sister. And she thinks she's frigid?

I want to show her how wrong she is. If she'll let me learn her body, I'll make her fly. But I need her relaxed and trusting first.

"So there's something I haven't told you," she says into the quiet elevator.

I turn my head to look at her and she's wringing her hands in front of her. "Whatever it is, it will be okay," I assure her.

"We'll see. So after you booked my flight I took the opportunity to book flights for Keller and Winnie. I didn't want to leave my sister in Big Wood to have to deal with the Bishops alone."

I nod.

"They're here. In our suite. I'm sorry, I should have told you. But I didn't want you to get mad."

"Mad?" I turn my entire body to face her. Then I cup her cheeks. "Wren, you never have to worry about that with me. Ever. This seems as good a time as any to get some things straight. I don't know what kind of shit show your marriage to Colt was, but undoubtedly ours will be different.

You are not alone anymore, if you need something you tell me. New clothes or Keller needs a new bike or even if you just need a hug, you come to me."

Her honey-colored eyes widen a little.

"You get me?"

"Yeah, I think so."

"About what I said right before our ceremony, I know you need more time. I respect that. I will be patient." The elevator stops and the doors slide open. I link our fingers together and lead her to our suite.

"I've waited this long, I can wait a little longer."

When we walk into the suite, her sister is standing in the kitchen. From the herbal aroma, I'm guessing she's making some hot tea.

"Congratulations you two," she whisper-yells.

"Is he already asleep?" Wren asks.

"Yeah, I think it was just walking through the casino. All the noises and sounds. By the time we got up here, he was tapped. Really loved the hamburger and milkshake though," Winnie says. She smiles at me. "Good to see you again, Liam."

I go to her and hug her. "You too, Winnie. Thanks for being here."

"Of course. You smell really good, by the way."

"Thanks."

"Before I head to bed myself, I got a nanny job."

Wren rushes to her sister and hugs her. "That's amazing."

"Yeah, I'm just glad to have something to start the summer with, so I didn't have to go work at that day camp. Mosquitos and heat are not my friends." She picks up her cup of tea and walks out of the kitchen, heading to the closed door. "Well, I'm going to sleep. Goodnight y'all."

I catch Wren shooting her sister daggers with her eyes, but miss what Winnie must be doing to get that reaction.

"Y'all have fun. Do all the things I haven't done," she singsongs as she steps into the bedroom.

"What does that mean?" I ask.

"Who knows? She's crazy." Wren tries to laugh things off, but she doesn't sound remotely amused.

"You want to shower first?" I ask her. Yes, I'd had visions of us showering together. I'd finally get a chance to wrap that gorgeous, long, brown hair around my hand.

"Yes, please."

"Want me to order anything up to eat or drink?"

She shakes her head. "It's been a long day, I think I just want to sleep." She hesitates for a moment, then says, "I actually need your help with something."

"Of course, anything."

She walks to me, then turns to give me her back. She holds those gorgeous brown waves out of the way. "Can you unzip me? Winnie helped me get dressed. I could ask her—"

"But I'm your husband," I tell her.

I pull the zipper that goes from the top of her neck down to almost her ass. The red, shimmery fabric gapes as I go. Revealing first a red bra and then red panties. I'm hard instantly.

I run the back of my hand down the length of her back, and she shivers beneath my touch. Leaning forward, I press a kiss to that spot where her shoulder meets her neck.

"Know this, wife. I will wait until you're ready, but once that time comes, I won't hold anything back. I'm going to claim every part of you."

chapter six

WREN

The last forty-eight hours have been a whirlwind. Starting with my phone call to Liam and ending with him driving me, my son, and my sister to my house in Big Wood.

Well, technically NOT my house, just where I've lived for the last eight years.

I'm worried about Keller. He's not used to so much stimulation all at one time. I keep expecting him to have an outburst, but he's been a complete champ. Las Vegas is definitely not made for kids on the spectrum with sensory processing issues. Thank God for noise-cancelling headphones.

Liam turns into the driveway, then frowns. He looks behind us, then at the house.

"This looks like you're practically in the Bishops' back yard," he says.

Winnie snorts. "Ya think?"

Super helpful, that one. I take a sobering breath, then open my car door.

"I'll take Keller to his room and start packing his stuff," my sister says.

"Thank you. Let me know if he needs me."

"Will do, but we'll be fine."

I nod. Liam grabs the big plastic totes from the back of the large SUV he rented.

Once we get inside, it's like I'm seeing the house for the first time. There's nothing in here that reflects me, save the family pictures on the refrigerator. Brenda never failed to mention how cluttered they made the kitchen look, but I didn't care.

I love all the pictures of my son growing up over the last seven years. And pictures of him with his dad. Some with me and Colt, too, back when things were better.

All of the furniture is high-end and frankly,

not very comfortable. Liam sets down the crates and separates them, tossing the lids to one corner in the living room.

"Hey Songbird? You okay?"

"Yeah, sure."

He walks to me and pulls me in for a hug. Those strong arms of his wrap around my body, pressing me tight to his. "It's okay to be sad. This has been your home."

I release a chuckle. "I'm not sad. Overwhelmed, maybe, not definitely not sad." I look up into his face—that gorgeous face and those dark as night brown eyes, the one-day stubble that's dark against his cheeks and chin. "I'm sorry you had to do this for us. I never want to be an inconvenience or a burden. But I need you to know how much I appreciate you sacrificing everything for me."

He pulls back a little, his hands gripping my biceps. He searches my face, his features drawn tight in a frown.

"Let's get one thing straight. I am not sacrificing anything. You and Keller becoming my family is a blessing. I promise you that." He stares into my eyes for a while before he speaks again. "Can I ask you a question?"

“Anything,” I say.

“Why did you ask me? I’m assuming you know other men who would’ve jumped at the chance to be your husband. Men you’ve seen more than a handful of times over the last several years.”

“I asked you because I trust you. I felt pretty certain you'd say yes because you're that guy. The reliable, steadfast one.”

“I said yes because I've always wanted to be something you need.”

When he says things like that, it makes my heart flutter with hope. I know Liam would never willingly hurt me, but I’d be a liar if I said I wasn’t afraid of that.

He kisses my forehead, then steps away from me. “Now then, I have the movers and moving truck scheduled for tomorrow.” He holds out a pad of brightly colored sticky notes. Stick one of these on any of the bigger pieces you want to bring with us.”

I stare down at the squares in my hand and then shake my head. I hold them back out to him.

“What’s the matter?” he asks.

"None of the things in this house are mine. Everything belongs to Brenda and Butch," I say.

Liam's frown deepens. "I don't understand. You have no pieces of furniture that you picked out? Or any you want to keep?"

"Even if I wanted to keep anything, which I do not, Brenda would have a fit."

"Why is it their stuff, though?"

"This marriage was very crowded. I don't think I have time to explain it right now. There's no doubt in my mind that they will have seen the car park in the driveway. Not to mention, they run the cameras at my doorbell and back door. So they'll know I'm back. They won't wait long to drive over here."

He rubs at the back of his neck. "They have the app linked to your doorbell camera?"

I nod. "I know, it sounds crazy. In any case, the number of missed calls and texts I've received from them—and their lawyer—in the last two days lets me know that they're watching. They knew I was gone. Didn't know where, but knew I'd taken Keller and left town. They're not pleased."

"Well too fucking bad," Liam says, his voice

dark and ominous. "You don't have to tell me everything now, but eventually I need to know."

"Why? None of it matters anymore," I say. "The attorney I spoke to made it clear that if I were married, they'd have no grounds for petitioning for full custody. No matter what they've been saying about me."

"It matters to me. I want to know what your life has been like since I foolishly left you here." He steps closer and lowers his voice. "I don't like to speak ill of the dead, but if Colt were alive right now I'd wring his damn neck."

I lean in and kiss his cheek. "I'll tell you everything you want to know, just not now."

"We've got a long drive from here back to Texas, so we'll have plenty of time to talk. Now tell me what we can pack."

"My clothes, I guess, though they're not exactly my style."

"Pick the ones you like or are most comfortable, and we'll buy you new stuff when we get home. What about Keller's things?"

"I mean, they bought him a lot of things over the years, but most of what they got him is in the garage. Guns and two different ATVs, lots of sporting equipment, that kind of thing.

"So basically all the stuff that he's clearly not into at all," Liam says.

How has he managed to know that about my son when they've only ever spent time together over a computer screen during video chats? "All of his favorite things are in his room. His puzzles, models, and building blocks. Winnie will know what to pack."

"Knock-knock," Brenda singsongs from the doorway.

"I'm guessing that happens frequently?" Liam says quietly. "The popping in without calling first?"

I just nod, then turn to face my mother-in-law. As usual, she's dressed in a pantsuit ala Hilary Clinton circa 2016. I told her that once, and I thought her head might explode. In any case, today's is peach. I hate peach; the color, the smell. She's probably why, considering she uses some fancy lotion and powder from France, I think, and it's all peach scented.

"Hello, Brenda," I say. Then I motion to Liam, who's now standing very close to me. The front of his body brushing against my behind. "You remember Liam."

At the mention of his name, he leans down and brushes a kiss against my neck.

And that's when Butch walks in. Unlike his wife, Butch likes to dress like a wealthy cowboy. Starched jeans, pointed boots in any kind of leather you can imagine. He must have sixty pairs. The button-down shirt and a belt buckle that would make Texas proud.

"What have we here?" he asks as he steps inside.

Liam pats me on the hip as he steps around me. He walks straight up to Colt's parents. "Mr. and Mrs. Bishop, so nice to see you again. It's been a while."

"It has been a *very* long while," Brenda says, emphasizing the 'very.'

"Liam was on active duty until just the last two years," I say. They can belittle me all they want, but I'll be damned if they discredit all of the sacrifices Liam has made.

"What is going on here?" Butch asks, clearly done with the charade of niceties.

Liam grabs my hand and brings it to his lips. "I finally convinced her to marry me. I've been asking for years, haven't I, baby?"

I smile up at him. "You sure have."

"Well, you'll have to get an annulment. She is a Bishop," Brenda says.

"Actually, now I'm a Gregory," I say. "And so is Keller, Liam's filed a petition in Texas to legally adopt him."

"Texas, why on Earth would he file there?" Butch asks.

"Because that's where I live, sir," Liam says. "Where my family will live with me."

"Now see here, son," Butch hits that last word hard. "We always did like you, Liam. We knew you were a good influence on our boy. But this," he wags his finger between Liam and me. "This is a goddamn mistake. You don't know what you're doing. I'm sure she's fed you so many lies, you don't know which way is up. Trust us, we know how she can be."

Panic claws at my throat with Butch's words. What if they convince Liam and he does annul our union? What will I do then? Flee the country, if possible.

"I'd remind you that you're in the presence of a lady, two if you count your wife," Liam says. "There's no need to use vulgarities."

Brenda steps forward. "You don't know how fragile and unstable she is. She needs us around to support her and Keller. She's just not up for raising a kid on her own. Especially with the medication," she whispers that last word like it's offensive, "she takes."

"Brenda, we've been over this. I take anxiety medication and something for my ADHD. It's not like I'm addicted to pain pills," I snap.

Brenda's eyes flash with anger, and she steps forward.

This time, Liam moves my body so I'm behind his.

"I'm here now, she's my wife, mine to care for. She won't need you anymore. But as far as I can tell, she has done better raising Keller alone these past few years than she was able to when Colt was alive. Because she had to take care of him too."

"If you think you're going to marry Wren just to get your hands on Colt's money, you're sorely mistaken! Keller's money is in a trust, and you'll never be able to touch it. And since Wren married you, she won't be getting anything from us anymore either," Brenda says.

"You expect us to believe you just appeared in her life and now you want to play family?" Butch asks.

"I'm not playing. I AM her family. And she and Keller are mine."

chapter seven

LIAM

After Butch and Brenda had stormed off with a "this isn't over!" threat, we'd made quick work of packing everything Wren wanted.

I hadn't intended for us to get on the road today, but I knew as soon as we had some miles between us and the Bishops, my girl would relax some.

What the fuck kind of crazy world has she been living the last several years? I had so many questions. Had things been different when Colt had been alive? Had he insulated her from his parents? Stood up to them?

What the hell did they even want with a gentle, sweet kid like Keller? He was the very antithesis of Colt.

I remember the Bishops being uppity and snobbish about their money. They'd liked me because I had a way of grounding Colt. He'd always been a bit of a wild child. They'd said he was precocious, but it had been more like rebelliousness than anything.

Wren was still wringing her hands in her lap as she stared out the window. The tall pine trees that lined the interstate as we crossed from Tennessee into Alabama made the road dark. I'd forgotten what these roads felt like. So much of Texas is spread out and wide where you can see miles at a time.

"I think I'm gonna find us a hotel," I say quietly.

"You must be so tired," she says.

In truth, I wasn't all that tired. My mind was far too occupied for that. But they needed to rest. In an actual bed.

"I think we could all use a hot shower and a nice bed."

"Sounds great." Wren peeked over her shoulder to check on her son.

We drove for another hour before I turned off in Tuscaloosa. I found us a hotel and booked adjoining rooms. She was unlikely to be ready to share a bed with me, but I wanted them close.

About forty-five minutes later, I'm showered and coming out of the bathroom with a towel around my hips. Wren steps into my room from our adjoining doors, then her eyes widen.

"I'm sorry, I didn't mean to intrude," she says.

"You can't intrude, Songbird, you're my wife." I go to my bag and grab a pair of boxer briefs, drop my towel, and pull them up. In the span of those actions, I hear a very distinct gasp come from Wren's lips. I turn to face her then.

Her eyes are wide, her mouth round in a silent 'o'. She's wearing an oversized t-shirt that looks older than me. I don't see any shorts or anything, but the shirt hangs down pretty low.

"Did you need something?" I ask her.

She steps closer to me. "I wanted to thank you for earlier."

"Earlier, when?"

"You didn't have to invite Winnie to come and live with us in Texas, but I really appreciate the gesture."

"I was serious. Your sister is always welcome in our home. Wren, I want you to be happy." I frown. "I'm pretty sure your life has had a considerable lack of joy and happiness these last several years. I want to make up for that."

She gives me a sad smile. "That's not your job."

"No, I think it might be."

She bites down on her bottom lip, but doesn't turn to go back into her room.

"Did you need something else?" To busy myself so I don't reach out and touch her the way every molecule in my body is screaming for me to do, I plug my phone in. "Remember what I told you, anything you need, you come to me."

Her inhale is sharp. "I was wondering if you could... if you would hold me for a little while?"

"I'll hold you for the rest of my life, Songbird. It would truly be my pleasure." I take her hand and lead her over to the small sofa. I sit, pull her down onto my lap, then wrap my arms around her body.

Fuck me if this doesn't feel like the most right thing in the whole world.

Her face nuzzles into my neck, the warmth of her breath a reminder that she's mine now. Eventually she'll give me all of her body, and then I'm coming for her heart. I won't settle until I have all of her.

"Were they always like that with you?" I ask.

"Not initially. Or maybe early on, I just didn't notice. They were very insistent that Colt and I marry when they found out I was pregnant."

Damn. And here I thought my buddy had wooed and won her. "I didn't realize you were pregnant when y'all got married."

She sits up a little so she can see my face. "I don't know that Colt was planning to ask me, and it wasn't really on my radar either. But Brenda and Butch were adamant that we marry. They didn't want any of their friends to 'talk' as they put it."

"They are stuck in a previous time." I rub circles on her lower back. "So, explain the house and furniture thing to me."

"They had built that house for Colt, and Brenda had decorated it and filled it with furniture that was either heirlooms or things she purchased. It was made quite clear when I moved in that everything was to be left alone."

"And you just went along with it? Colt never told her no?"

She shrugs. "Colt would never say anything to his parents. I mean, he didn't obey their wishes for him, but that was never discussed. We all pretended that Colt didn't get hooked on those pain pills after his motorcycle accident. Hell, I think they pretended the accident hadn't even happened. For me, it was like living on the inside of a snow globe. Things would get shaken up, but then everything would fall right back into place to make a pretty scene. Nothing was real. Except for Keller."

That makes her smile, and the transformation on her face is breathtaking. I can't help it, so I reach out and touch her face. "You're so beautiful, Wren."

"Thank you," she says. "They wouldn't allow me to get a job. I mean, I wanted to stay home with Keller, especially once I realized that he had slightly different needs than a neurotypical kid would."

That makes me smile. "He's an amazing kid. When you fell asleep briefly in the car, he was telling me all about these robots he can build with his LEGO bricks. After that, he told me the capital cities of all the countries in South America. He's smarter than I am. I don't think I knew Uruguay was a country."

"And you're smiling about it," she says.

"Of course I am. I'm in awe of what a great job you've done raising him. Especially in the environment y'all have been in. You must be so proud of him. I feel proud, and I didn't have anything to do with it. He's truly a great kid."

She throws her arms around my neck. "Thank you for seeing him and not thinking he should be fixed or different in any way."

"He's perfect just the way he is." We stay this way for a while, her clinging to me and me rubbing her back. But some of my questions can't wait. I shift her on my lap so she's facing me, her thighs on the outside of my thighs. "Did Colt ever hurt you, Wren? Will you tell me that much?"

She licks her lips. "He never hit me, if that's what you're asking. He was indifferent mostly, selfish and self-centered. Once I knew he was sleeping with other women, I kicked him out of our bedroom. Well, really, I just moved myself into the bedroom next to Keller's. We shared the Jack-and-Jill bathroom."

"And the drugs?"

"Mostly OxyContin. That's what he died from. Too many of those mixed with vodka. I don't think it was intentional. He just had no limitations. He was a spoiled child." She lifts a shoulder as if that explains everything.

"Why didn't you ever just leave him?"

"I wanted to. Planned to even. But the lawyer I spoke to was a friend of a friend of Butch's and soon enough they came knocking to tell me what would happen if I left their son. Threats. So many years of threats to take my son away." She shakes her head. "It was exhausting. That's the best way to describe the entirety of my twenties. I mean aside from Keller and Winnie."

I stare into her beautiful face. Those honey-gold eyes, her full lips, the pile of brown waves looped in a messy bun, and her abundant curves. She'd been curvy back in high school, but now she had this lush softness that made me want to do wicked things to her. To watch all of those thick curves jiggle when I pounded into her. Fuck, as if I wasn't already fighting a hard-on with her snuggled on my lap.

My hands go to her hips. It's easy enough to

tell that she's not wearing shorts, just panties under that t-shirt.

I know I shouldn't ask because I likely don't want to hear the answer. Still, I find myself asking, "Did you love him?"

"At one time, I did, I think. But it feels like it was another lifetime." She takes a breath. "I don't think I'm the same woman now that I was then."

"Probably not. I know I'm not the same guy who left all those years ago to join the Army. Kinda like one of those rock tumblers, only in reverse. You put the shiny, fresh rock inside, then life rumbles and tumbles, knocking you against surfaces until you come out jagged and a little dull- looking."

"That's exactly what it's like. Never thought about it that way before." Her eyes flick to my lips.

I want to squeeze her hips and pull her pussy flush against my cock which is now hard and stiff in my boxers. If she looked down at my lap, at the space between our bodies, she'd see it clearly outlined by the tight cotton.

"What if you don't like the me that I am today?" she whispers.

"Impossible. You'll always be my favorite person, no matter how you change."

Her eyes once again drop to my lips. This time, I lean up to meet her, and our mouths crash in the middle. Lips and tongues, our kisses are heated and full of pent-up desire. I squeeze her hips and pull her against me. The heat from her pussy hits my dick and I groan.

And still we kiss. I lift one hand and bring it up to cup her tit, over her shirt. Copping a feel while we're making out, like I always wanted to do in high school. Her nipple is already hard, and she arches into my touch. The movement drags her pussy against my cock.

She feels good. She tastes good. I want nothing more than to pull our underwear aside and sink into her slick heat.

"Fuck, Wren, you have no idea how long I've wanted you in my arms like this." I kiss and lick down the column of her throat.

"Liam, you feel good." Her words come out a little breathy.

I rock myself up, loving the friction we're creating.

She takes the hand on her tit and lowers it enough to lift the hemline of her shirt. Then I'm snaking my palm against her hot, naked skin. When I touch her breast like this, we both moan. She's fucking perfect.

Her mouth finds mine again, and her tongue slicks against mine. And fuck I'm already feeling close enough to come.

I tweak her nipple, pinching and tugging on it lightly, finding the things she likes. Her hands find my shoulders and she shamelessly works her body against mine.

Then she shudders against me as an orgasm rocks through her body. And I come too because it's the hottest thing I've ever seen.

She pulls back from my lips, her eyes are wide and her mouth is open. "Oh God. I can't believe that just happened."

"You made me come in my boxers," I tell her with a grin.

"I did? Oh."

"You're gorgeous when you come, wife. It's going to be my new hobby, finding all the ways and places I can bring you to climax."

chapter **eight**

WREN

By the time we pull into the driveway to Liam's house the next day, I'm ready to run around the block to stretch my legs. But I am not a runner by anyone's standards.

Keller has been excitedly chattering for the last hour, eager to see our new home.

"Try to remember that Liam didn't have time to get things ready for us because we moved so fast. We'll get your room set up just right later."

"I know, Mom. I can roll with it."

That makes me chuckle, and Liam laughs as

well. Making us both laugh has my son smiling so big.

While my sweet boy is thinking about our new home, my brain keeps replaying what happened last night. All the kissing. The grinding. The orgasm that hit me out of nowhere. I've had a few before, always with a toy, though, so to say I was surprised would be an understatement.

And he'd climaxed too. Remembering that now makes desire pull low through my belly. I definitely am attracted to Liam. No big surprise there, he's gorgeous. But I am surprised at how much I actually do want to have sex with him.

Everything he did to me last night—and let's face it, we were basically like two teenagers doing some heavy petting—felt amazing. Like he knew precisely where and how to touch me. He hadn't even been trying to get me off, at least I don't think so.

I should text Winnie and see what she thinks.

"Okay, we're here," Liam says. "Who wants to never get in a car again?"

"Me!" Keller says.

"Me too, bud. My legs are toast."

"Liam, your legs are made up of sinew,

bones, tendons, ligaments, and a plethora of blood vessels. Not crunch bread," my son says.

I suppress a smile and see Liam looking at me. "What? I mean, he's not wrong."

"No, he's not. You're going to teach me about all kinds of things, aren't you, Keller?"

"We might want to start with basic anatomy because it seems like you might have been misled at some point in your education."

That makes Liam laugh even harder. The rich rumble of the sound is nearly the best thing I've ever heard. And it hits me... we could be happy here. Keller and I could make a home with Liam, and maybe someday we'll be a real family.

"Come on, you two, let me show you the house." He grabs my hand, threading our fingers together, and we follow behind my son as he heads to the front door. "He's hilarious," Liam mouths to me.

"Yes, he is. But it's not always intentional. He doesn't always catch sarcasm or satire."

He nods. "Me neither."

I squeeze his hand to let him know how much I appreciate the way he's been with Keller. I've never seen Keller open up to someone as quickly as Liam. Yes, they'd "met" a couple of times on video chat, but overall, they haven't had much interaction. But somehow Liam knows exactly how to talk to my son.

Certainly more than Keller's father ever did.

The house is a dark color, maybe blue, with white trim. It's a single-story ranch-style, with several large windows across the front.

Liam quickly points out the bathrooms first so we can all have a quick potty break before we get an official tour. Then the three of us head down one hallway to Keller's room. My son goes in first after Liam turns on the lights.

"Mom, you said it wouldn't be ready. But it is. You were kidding with me, weren't you?" Keller asks.

I stare, open-mouthed probably, at the room that's decorated perfectly for my son. There's even a wall that the lower half is covered in LEGO baseplates so he can build right on the wall.

Keller is busy exploring where he'll be able to put his books and puzzles. I grab Liam's hand and squeeze.

"How?" I ask him.

He smiles. "I'll tell you later."

“Do I have to go on the rest of the house tour, or can I stay in here?” Keller asks.

“You can stay in here, bud,” Liam says. “It’s not a super big house, so I don’t think you’ll get lost. I’m going to show your mom our room next, which is all the way on the other side of the house. So if you need us, just go back out into the hallway and keep walking until you find us.”

Keller nods, and Liam leads me out and down the hall.

“Seriously, how did you do that?” I ask.

“I had some of the guys from work set it up.”

I stop walking and turn to face him. “Why would you do that?”

Surprise flashes across his features, then he frowns. “I wanted him to walk into the house and feel comfortable. I wanted him to feel like that room was his from the moment he arrived. I know we have a lot of work to do to make this house a family home, but I knew the very first priority was Keller’s room.”

“But how did ‘the guys’ know what to do?”

“I sent them detailed instructions. I was their team leader, they know how to follow orders.”

I raise up on my tip-toes and press my mouth

to his. “Thank you. You do not know how much that means to me.”

“Maybe now you’ll start believing that I’ll do anything for you, especially if you thank me with kisses. And you’re very welcome.”

I can’t help but smile. Winnie was right, I do still love Liam. I’m not sure if it ever went away or if he somehow managed to get me to fall in love with him all over again in the last three days.

He leads me the rest of the way to his bedroom—our bedroom, I guess. It’s a sizable room with a bay window to the right. There’s not one there now, but definite space for a bench. It would be a perfect reading nook.

Wow, I’m already mentally re-decorating, and I haven’t even seen most of the house.

The king-sized bed is on the far wall, flanked by wall sconces. Basic white bedding covers the bed. There are two doors to our left.

“This is the bathroom. It’s got a great tub if you still like to soak in the tub and read,” he says.

“How do you even remember that?” I once asked Colt to pick up my favorite bath bombs, and he had no idea what I was talking about.

Stop comparing them!

It's pointless. There is no comparison, I knew that before I married Colt. Before I slept with him too.

"Because I listen, Songbird," Liam says. "You're important to me, so I pay attention and remember."

I am in so much trouble here. Liam has the power to annihilate my poor, bruised heart. I don't think he would do it on purpose, but it could still happen. Would I be able to pick up the pieces like I had to after Colt died?

"Also, a shower and two sinks. I was told the double sinks are a marriage saver," he tells me with a wink.

He walks to the other door and opens it, then flips on the lights. "I told the guys to move my stuff around in here so you get most of the space."

I follow him into a huge walk-in closet. It's already set up with hanging bars, as well as shelves, and a floor-length mirror hangs on one wall.

"Holy giant closet, Batman!" I say.

He laughs. "Yeah. I picked this house because of the back yard, but the other amenities didn't hurt. It was originally built in the sixties, but was completely updated and upgraded a couple of years ago."

"It's amazing. The closet and everything else I've seen. You're amazing." I blurt out that last bit and then wince because that was totally random.

But Liam just smiles and walks closer to me. "I'm glad you think so, wife. I happen to think you're amazing as well." He leans in and runs his nose up the side of my throat. "I can't stop thinking about last night. How you looked falling apart on my lap. Fuck, Wren, you have no idea how much I want you."

My nipples are like diamonds, they're so hard. "I might know a little," I admit. "If it's how much I want you." I'm not sure where the bravery comes from that allows me to admit that. Maybe it's the lack of sleep. Or finally being in another state away from my nightmarish in-laws. Or maybe it's just Liam.

Sweet, reliable, sexy as hell, Liam.

"Are you going to let me touch you tonight?" he asks.

"Maybe."

"Maybe is a lot better than no." He kisses me

briefly, just teasing my lips with a swipe of his tongue.

My pussy tightens and arousal floods my panties.

"Mom, you gotta see this!" Keller's voice comes from the bedroom.

I release a pent-up breath and step out of the closet. "What is it?"

"There's a LEGO wall in my room!"

"I saw that. Isn't it the coolest?" His excitement is palpable. I wrap my son in my arms. "I love you."

"Love you," he says. "Liam, did you see the LEGO wall?"

"I did, bud, and you know what else?"

"What?" Keller asks.

"I think there might be some new LEGO kits in your closet."

Keller's mouth drops open. Then he runs from the room.

I laugh. "Well, we won't see him for several hours. He locks in on those."

"Oh, maybe I shouldn't have told him until tomorrow. I don't want to mess with his bedtime or whatever."

“He slept a lot in the car. So it’s okay for tonight.”

“How about I show you the rest of the house?”

chapter
nine

WREN

ME: He made me come!

WINNIE: WHAT?!

WINNIE: Details, woman.

ME: In the hotel room last night. We were making out, and I was sitting on his lap.

WINNIE: Dry humping? Please tell me it was dry humping!

ME: Seriously, why are you like this?

ME: <laugh emoji>

ME: Yes, that's totally what it was.

WINNIE: That's so hot. It's the Big D Energy!

ME: It's not just energy.

WINNIE: I knew it!

ME: Okay, but from now on, you can't be thinking about his Big D, energy, or otherwise. Because he's my husband.

WINNIE: Meow. Kitty has some claws, I see. Ready to admit that you still love him?

ME: Yeah, you were right about that too.

ME: He's said some things too. These little comments.

ME: I don't know. I'm probably reading into things too much.

WINNIE: Riding that orgasm high.

ME: Something like that.

WINNIE: What are the things he's said that you're overanalyzing?

ME: That he's going to claim me. All of me.

WINNIE: Why is that caveman talk so damn hot?

ME: Don't know, but it totally is.

WINNIE: What else?

ME: That he's waited for me.

ME: That anything I need, I go to him. Anything.

ME: Other things too, but now my brain isn't working.

ME: But do you know what he did?

WINNIE: Aside from melting your brain with an orgasm?

ME: Rude.

ME: But yes.

ME: He had his friends set up Keller's room before we got here. A bed, a LEGO wall, and places for his books and puzzles, and new LEGO sets.

WINNIE: I'm not crying. You're crying.

ME: I know. My poor, dumb heart didn't stand a chance.

WINNIE: This is what you've deserved all along. A man who will take care of you and love your son.

ME: I think I'm gonna sleep with him tonight.

WINNIE: Sleep?

ME: No.

WINNIE: Ride 'em, Cowgirl!

ME: I hate you.

WINNIE: No, you don't.

WINNIE: Before you go get naked and dirty with your hot husband…

WINNIE: I started my nanny job today.

ME: How'd it go?

WINNIE: He fired me.

ME: What?

WINNIE: Well, he tried to fire me, but his daughter, Clementine (OMG how cute is she?!), already loved me and told him he couldn't.

ME: So is he a jackass?

WINNIE: He's a big ol' grump. Hot AF, but a grumpy ass.

chapter ten

LIAM

I finish giving Wren a tour of the house, and we go check on Keller again. He's so focused on building one of his new LEGO kits, he doesn't even notice us in the doorway.

"Keller, do you want to save the rest of the building for tomorrow and you can go to sleep?" Wren asks.

He looks up at his mother with an expression of incredulity. "Mom, I'm in the zone now."

She laughs. "I thought as much. Just wanted to ask. Is it okay if I go to bed?"

"Course," he says, his attention back on the multi-colored blocks in his hand. The instruction manual is on the floor next to him.

"You know where to find me if you need me?" she asks.

"Yep."

"Do you have your water bottle?"

"Yes, Mom. Already filled it in the kitchen." He points behind him, and sure enough, the blue water bottle with his name on it sits on the bedside table.

Wren laughs. "Well, okay then. I'll see you in the morning. I love you."

"Love you too," he says. "You too, Liam."

That gets me right in the feels. My throat tightens with emotion, and I nod. "I love you, Keller," I tell him. It's the easiest thing in the world, loving him, next to loving his mom.

Wren grabs my hand and squeezes it, then pulls on it.

"Let's go to our room," she says quietly.

She doesn't have to ask me twice. So we leave the seven- year-old to his building and head down the hallway.

Once we're enclosed in the bedroom, Wren

presses up against me and kisses me. My hands go to her ass and squeeze. I change our positions so she's the one against the door. I lift her, and her legs wrap about my waist. I'm already so damn hard.

And then I remember something I need to come clean about. I pull back from our kiss and walk us over to the bed. "I don't want there to be any lies or untruths between us," I say as I sit on the edge of the mattress.

She frowns.

"So I have a confession before we go any further."

She swallows visibly and nods. "Whatever you have to say, I can take it."

Her words are like a kick to my gut. I hate that Colt and his parents took her confidence and whittled it down to nearly nothing.

"Whatever you're thinking, it's wrong. This isn't about you." I search her face. "After we got married the other night, and we were in the car going back to the hotel. I eavesdropped on your texting conversation with Winnie."

Her lips part, but she says nothing.

"It was rude of me to do, but being able to

decipher words in the reflection of glass is a handy skill in the work I used to do."

"So you saw me admit I'd never had an orgasm with a man," she says.

I give her a wicked grin. "You can't say that anymore, can you?"

"No, I suppose I can't."

"So first, let me apologize for reading your conversation without you knowing. Secondly, you are not frigid. Not by any means. I even want to be sorry that Colt was such a shitty lover to you, but I can't find it in myself to feel that. Because all I feel, all I can think about is the fact that I get to have so many of your firsts."

"My firsts?" she asks.

"I got your first climax with a partner last night."

She nods.

"Now I can start collecting the rest. The first time I make you come on my tongue."

She sucks in a breath and her eyes go a shade darker.

"The first time you come on my cock. The first time you sit on my face."

"Liam," she whispers.

"The first time I make you scream my name.

Come on my fingers. Really, the possibilities are limitless. But I didn't want to make love to you before I came clean about that. I will try not to secretly read your texts again."

"I'm not mad," she says.

But I sense she's not saying everything on her mind. "What else?"

"What if you're wrong and I can't come in all those ways? What if it's not you, but it's my body not cooperating?"

"I'm not worried about it. Just because your first husband didn't take the time to get to know your body, doesn't mean I'm not going to do everything possible to learn how to make your body sing. This isn't something for me to get frustrated about. Knowing I can touch you, kiss you, fuck you, is all the pleasure I need. I will enjoy whatever efforts I put in to get you there."

"Are you sure?"

"Fuck yeah, I'm sure." I kiss her forehead. "But I also need to say, and I'm annoyed with myself for even mentioning this. If you need more time, I can wait until you're ready."

"You said you'd waited for me for a while."

I nod.

"What did you mean by that?"

"Oh, Songbird, surely you know I've been in love with you since high school. Hell, you're the reason I joined the Army."

"I'm sorry, what?"

"Unfortunately, the logic of an eighteen-year-old boy insisted I go away and make something of myself before I'd be worthy of you."

"To quote one of my favorite movies, 'you about done?'"

"What movie?"

"Sweet Home Alabama. The point is, you've always been worthy. You didn't need to do anything or change to be with me."

"Yeah, I figured that out eventually. About the time I heard the news that you married my best friend."

She winces.

"It was my own fault. I waited. I left."

"And that was before Colt's accident. Before he became a selfish husk of the man he'd been before. I mean we had no business sleeping together. The only thing we ever had in common was you. I won't regret my life with Colt. I can't. I wouldn't have my son and I wouldn't trade him for anything."

"Me neither. I think how it happened is how it was meant to be," I say.

"While we're being honest... " she says, then pauses. "I want to admit something. "I'm scared, Liam. Scared of letting myself love you, scared of letting myself be loved by you, scared for my son. I'm so tired of being hurt and let down by the people who are supposed to love me."

I cup her cheeks. "Songbird, I will never hurt you. Ever. I'd rather cut off my own arm. That goes for Keller too. Speaking of, I hope it's not too presumptuous of me to have already initiated adoption papers for him. I figured that would be the very best way to insulate y'all from a custody issue."

Her eyes widen and fill with tears. "You already filed for that? I know I said that to the Bishops, but that was just me talking, trying to scare them into canceling their custody case."

"I know because we hadn't really talked about it. But I still want to do it."

"How do you know that's even what you want?"

"Of course it's what I want, you and Keller are my family. I made vows in a creepy little chapel, I intend to stick with them."

She gives me a watery laugh. "I would like for my husband to make love to me now."

"You don't have to ask me twice." I kiss her then, pouring all my feelings into her. I've loved this woman for the majority of my life and I finally get to show her.

chapter **eleven**

WREN

"Get undressed, Songbird. You have no idea how badly I am dying to see all that creamy flesh, all those fucking curves."

I swallow thickly, but do what he says. First my jeans and then my t-shirt, until I'm standing in just my bra and panties.

Liam's still in his jeans, though they're undone and barely clinging to his hips. The outline of him straining against his briefs makes my throat go dry. When he dropped the towel in the hotel room and I got an amazing view of his perfect ass, I thought I might die. But now I get to touch him.

I slide my hand up the firm planes of his chest, letting my palms map out the ridges of his abs. He's Michelangelo's David come to life, but warm and alive under my touch. Dark hair dusts across his pecs before narrowing into a perfect line trailing below his waistband. I follow it with a single finger, dipping just my fingertip into the waistband of his boxers.

"Your body is insane," I tell him. "Makes me feel stupid.

His breath hitches. "Good to know. Because I'm pretty sure I've lost countless brain cells fantasizing about yours."

I slip my fingers under the waistband of his underwear, and he lets out a sharp hiss.

"Fuck, Songbird," he growls, his voice husky. "You have no idea how good that feels. Makes me want to do unspeakable things to you."

My pulse kicks, desire pools low in my belly. "Like what?"

"I want to spend hours with my face between those thick thighs. I want to fuck you in every position imaginable. I want to wrap your gorgeous hair around my fist while I fuck your mouth. Do you want me to go on?"

"I want you to take off your jeans," I say.

"Yes, ma'am. Get on the bed though."

I do as I'm told. "I'm just ready, that's all I know."

"You've been starved for affection for so long, my beautiful Wren. I'm going to make you forget what being hungry felt like. From now on, when you need to be touched, no matter day or night, you come to me. I will always take care of your needs."

If a woman could come from words alone, those would have pushed me over the edge.

He shoves his boxer briefs down, and I get my first full look at his dick. He's long, thick, and heavy with need—he's everything I'd imagined and so much more.

He crawls into bed beside me, half covering me, bracing his weight on his forearm as his mouth finds mine. His kiss is heat and hunger and reverence all in one. By the time he pulls back, I'm soaked and aching for him.

"Liam, please, I need you. I don't think I've ever been this wet."

His body settles between my thighs, and I feel the full weight of him. I gasp.

"You have me, Wren," he says. "All of me. I've always belonged to you."

I wrap my arms around him, pulling him closer, wanting to climb inside this moment and live in it forever. We kiss again, and it's all-consuming—sweet and savage all at once. I rock my hips upward, desperate for more friction, more contact.

"I'm going to mark off one of those firsts now and make you come before I sink inside of you."

He slides two fingers inside me, and I arch into him with a moan.

"Goddamn, Wren, you're drenched." His voice is edged with reverence.

His thumb brushes over my clit in a circular motion.

"Don't think," he says. "Just feel. My cock is already dripping for you, ready to be sheathed inside your wet heat."

"Oh God," I groan. Everything inside me is tightening.

"Yeah, you like the idea of me wanting you

that badly? Did you like it the other night when you made me come in my pants like a damn horny teen?"

"Yes," I hiss.

His fingers are patient as he works my body with a touch so exact, it feels like we've always been doing this.

Then my body clenches. Spins, and then breaks apart.

"God, watching you fall apart is the sexiest thing I've ever seen," he groans. Then he curses.

"What?"

"I don't have a condom."

"I'm on birth control," I say quickly. "Have been for years. You don't need one. And I got tested after I found out Colt was cheating. I never let him touch me after that."

Relief floods his features. "I haven't been with anyone in years. Haven't wanted to."

"Make me yours completely, Liam."

He lowers himself down, positioning his dick at my entrance. When he finally pushes inside, I gasp. He's definitely stretching me. I'm full in a way I've never been and everything about it feels right and perfect.

"You were made for me," he says through gritted teeth. "Fuck, Songbird, how are you still so fucking tight? "

"I had a C-section with Keller and Colt was no where near as big as you. In length or girth."

He laughs and it makes his cock vibrate inside me. I hike my legs up and wrap them around his hips.

His thrusts are slow at first, then they become stronger, harder, faster.

"Yes," I whisper.

"Fuck me. I want to fill you up, wife. I want to paint the insides of your womb with my seed and make sure everyone knows who you belong to."

"Yes, yes, do all of that." Somehow the base of his cock is hitting my clit with every thrust and it doesn't take long before I'm having the orgasm to end all orgasms. "I'm coming!"

"Yeah, I feel you. Squeezing me so goddamn good." He thrusts once, twice more—and then I feel him spill inside me, his groan muffled against my throat. It's the most intimate thing I've ever experienced.

"Holy shit, that was unreal," I say.

“If you’re still not a true believer, we’ll have to do it again.”

“Oh, in that case, yes, I will require some more evidence before I’m a true believer.”

chapter twelve

LIAM

Gravel crunches beneath the tires of my extended cab as I turn into the makeshift parking lot at Great Dane's Dog Sanctuary.

"This is amazing, Liam," Wren says, looking around.

"Yeah, we've made a lot of progress in the last several months, but the infrastructure is taking longer than we'd like. We've got all the pens set up. When we get any new dogs, they're quarantined for a while until we have them see the vet and get their vaccines. Then we start to socialize them in small groups before we let them loose in the big pen with the pack."

"Pack," she says with a snort. "Sounds like a wolf shifter romance."

"You read a lot of those?" I can't help but ask.

"I prefer bear shifters, actually. But historical romance will always be my favorite." She smiles at me. "Tell me more."

"Beau has worked hard to get the agility courses set up for the different sizes of dogs. Flynn and Jack have worked countless hours designing and building the actual buildings. We needed a shelter where the dogs could go to get away from inclement weather. And just the hot-as-actual-Hell Texas sun. Those were the structures we built first.

"Once Dane and Shelby's house was finished, we converted his tiny home into the main office. It's tight quarters, but it works for now."

"How many dogs do you have?"

"At any given moment, we have upwards of sixty, but we have capacity for eighty. We like to keep space open in case we have any emergencies. Like we had a truck come in a few months ago, basically an entire shelter's dog population. They were evacuating for a hurricane. Thankfully, that shelter sustained minimal damage, and the dogs were able to return a week later."

"I'm impressed," she says. "And amazed. You've not only created something incredible for the dogs, you've given your entire team a purpose. That's no small thing."

"I'm just in it for the dogs," I tell her with a wink. I put the truck in park and turn to face Keller. "You ready to go see the dogs, bud?"

Keller looks up at me, his eyes so much like his mother's, and he just shrugs.

"The Bishops were never fans of pets so we've never had an animal in the house. So he's never really been around them."

"Ah." Fucking Bishops. I make a mental note to see if Flynn can do some of his hacking magic on them. People that nasty have to be doing something illegal. Probably not, but you never know. "Well, don't worry, Keller, all of the dogs are behind fences. So you can decide how much interaction you want to have with them."

The main gate is already open, and some of the guys—Dane, Jack, Flynn, and Beau—are milling around near the training pens, waving when they see us. I step out and round the truck, opening Keller's door.

Keller's eyes dart to the giant fenced area where several dogs are already running and barking. "They're so big," he says quietly.

"Some of them, yeah. But you don't have to go in yet. We'll start slow." I offer him my hand. "Come on, buddy. Let's go say hi from the safe side first."

He takes my hand, still a little hesitant. Wren walks close on his other side, her free hand brushing his back. She smiles at me and I want to tell her how much I love her. How hard I'm going to work to make sure she and Keller are happy. I sure as fuck hope I'm enough for them.

The dogs go wild when we approach the fence. Tails wag, tongues loll, and one particularly enthusiastic mutt, a lab mix named Porkchop, does a triple spin before flopping onto his back for belly rubs.

"They know you," Keller says, looking up at me.

I grin. "They'd greet you the same if you worked here too."

Wren crouches by the fence, fingers extended through the open holes of the chain-link. A redbone coonhound named Mabel snuffles her hand and gives a low, happy huff.

"I love her," Wren says simply.

"Mabel loves everyone. She's a total sweetheart."

But Keller doesn't go any closer. He hangs back, chewing his lip.

"It's okay, bud," I tell him. "We've got a smaller space for meeting new friends. Wanna check that out instead?"

He nods quickly.

I lead them around to the side pen, which we use for testing therapy dogs. Only three dogs are inside—Blue, a patient terrier mix with one white ear; Banjo, a sleepy-eyed golden; and Franny, a small mutt with expressive eyebrows.

"They don't jump?" Keller asks.

"Nope. These guys are pros and they've been trained not to jump." I open the gate and hold it. "You want to go in with me?"

He pauses. Looks at Wren, who gives him a soft nod.

"I'll be right here the whole time," she tells him.

Then he walks in, slow and unsure, but moving.

Banjo ambles over first, fluffy tail wagging gently. She sniffs Keller's knee and sits.

Keller's eyes go wide. "I think she's waiting for me to pet her. Do you think so?"

"Yeah. She's really polite like that. And she loves attention."

"Watch," I tell him. I get down on one knee and scratch Banjo between the ears. "If you pet her here," I point to her chest, "she smiles." So I demonstrate, scratching the golden retriever's soft fur on her chest. Her mouth opens in what looks like a smile.

Tentatively, Keller reaches out, and when Banjo leans into his touch, Keller's face splits into a grin. The kind of grin you make a mental snapshot of because you want to remember it forever.

Blue joins a moment later, curling up in a patch of sun. Franny trots over and drops a slobbery tennis ball at Keller's feet.

"Franny likes to play," I tell him. "She wants you to throw the ball."

Keller looks at the ball and shakes his head.

I laugh. "I don't blame you. They're slimy sometimes." I pick up the dirt and slobber-covered tennis ball and toss it. Franny happily runs after it.

We stay in that pen for a while, letting Keller get comfortable. Wren's got her arms folded over the fence, watching with a look that's all soft affection.

When Keller kneels to scratch under Blue's chin, I clear my throat. "Got a big question for you, bud."

He glances up.

"You want to bring one of these pups home?"

His brow furrows. "Home?"

"Yeah. You can pick one to come live with us."

He looks genuinely confused. "But... they live here."

I crouch beside him. "They do, for now. But this isn't forever. It's just a place where we keep them safe and loved until their real family comes."

He blinks at me. "So we'd be their real family?"

"Exactly."

He glances at the three dogs. Franny's chewing the tennis ball to shreds, Blue's still snoozing, and Banjo is staring up at him like he hung the moon.

"I think... I think maybe we're Banjo's real family. Can we take her home?" he asks.

I wrap an arm around his small shoulders and pull him close. "I think you're right. I think she belongs with us." I glance over at my wife to see her wiping her cheeks. "What do you think, Songbird?"

She gives me a watery laugh and shrugs. "I think we might be a real family."

chapter thirteen

WREN

We're driving back to the house, Keller in the backseat with our new dog. I glance over at my husband. The man who made me climax no fewer than four times last night.

He and my sister were right, I'm not frigid.

That and I'm pretty sure Liam might be a sex expert. He's a sexpert. I snort.

"What are you laughing about?" he asks.

"I'll tell you later. It's not really for small ears." I look to the backseat again, where Keller is busy telling Banjo all about her new home.

"I think she loves me, Mom," Keller says, his voice filled with wonder.

"I think she definitely does."

"I want her to sleep in my room. Not in my bed, but maybe beside my bed. On the floor. Can she do that, Liam? Can Banjo sleep in my room?"

"It's okay with me, bud. But your mama has the final say."

Keller's eyes flick to my face. "Yes, it's okay with me. But if you change your mind, that's okay too." My son nods, then goes back to talking to the dog, now telling her all about his awesome room.

"You know, you don't need to buy his affection. He genuinely likes you, I can tell."

"Is that what you think? That's not at all it. Remember when I said I picked that house because of the backyard?"

"Yes."

"It's made for a dog. I even have everything already bought at home. It's just been in the garage waiting for me to pick a pup and bring them home. But letting Keller pick made more sense to me. I guess I should have asked you about it first?"

"Oh, that's not what I mean. I just want you to know that we're all in this too."

"Oh yeah? Like a real family?" His eyes flash when he repeats my earlier words.

"Yeah, just like that," I say.

"Speaking of our family, is it too soon to ask if you are interested in adding to our merry band?" he asks.

"Another dog?"

"Or another," his eyes flick to his rearview mirror.

"Another kid? Oh, yeah, I'd love to have more kids. It just wasn't an option in our previous life. BL, if you will."

"BL? What's that mean?" he asks.

"Before Liam."

He laughs at that. "Is that what we're going to call it?"

"That's what I'm calling it. I can already tell I'm healing, changing, and we're not even a full week into our marriage."

"So is my plan working?"

"What's your plan?"

"To make you happy," he says simply. "To make sure that you smile and laugh every day. To keep you safe. To make you feel loved and cherished. All of that goes for Keller too." Then he mouths, "and to make you come as many times as possible on a daily basis."

I laugh. "It's a solid plan, I like it."

We sit in companionable silence for the rest of the ride home. Once we get there, the boys take Banjo into the backyard to show the pup her new outdoor space.

I decide to go back to the bedroom and try to finish unpacking my clothes. I probably should try and buy some new things. I'm definitely looking forward to getting to know my new hometown.

I'm in the closet hanging up dresses when Liam calls my name.

"I'm in here," I tell him.

He appears in the doorway and leans against the frame; he gives me a wicked grin that makes my panties wet. Good grief, it's like he turned on my horny switch.

"How'd it go?" I ask.

"Great. Banjo loves the yard. Keller thinks he might want some gloves to play fetch with her."

That makes me laugh. "Sounds about right. You know, even as a baby, he didn't like his hands to get dirty."

"I mean, he's not wrong. Touching those slobber-covered tennis balls is gross. I think I'll wait a few weeks before I introduce him to the joys of scooping up the poop from the yard so you don't step on it."

"Yeah, you definitely want to wait on that. And maybe don't hold your breath on him helping."

"It's all good. It's not as nasty with the help of the long-handled tools. Fuck, why are we talking about dog shit?"

I shrug. "You brought it up."

"I did."

"Did you need something?" I ask.

"Yeah, I need you." He comes into the closet and pulls me into his arms.

The dress and hanger in my hands squish between our bodies.

"I'm in love with you, Wren Gregory, I hope you know that."

"I love you too, Liam. I always have."

"Oh yeah?"

"Yeah. I know I'm not the same person you fell in love with so long ago. The last decade of my life has shaped me in a way that doesn't always make me proud. Oddly enough, just being near you makes me feel like I'm healing though. But it might take a while. Are you sure I'm not too broken and damaged for you?"

"No. Never. You are everything. Its always been you, Songbird. Even when I wasn't supposed to want you, I still did. Now I get to call you mine. Forever."

"Forever?"

"Yep. No take backs. We made vows."

"In that creepy chapel?"

"Exactly. Vows made in creepy chapels last the longest. I think I read that somewhere."

I laugh. "Are you sure about that?"

"Most definitely." His hands slide down to my hips. "So, Keller is showing Banjo the wonders of a brand-new LEGO kit. That should buy us enough time for me to fuck you at least once."

"At least," I agree.

"Then let's get started."

chapter **fourteen**

LIAM

ME: Thanks for not being total asshats when I brought Wren and Keller by today.

JACK: When are we ever asshats?

DANE: That might apply to everyone but you, Jack.

JACK: Does that make me the pussy of the group?

DANE: No. Just the golden retriever.

ROMEO: Dane is not wrong.

ROMEO: Your bird girl is perfect for you.

BEAU: Bird girl?

ME: Romeo is just being his hilarious self.

ROMEO: Because her name is wren. Like a bird.

BEAU: That's weak, dude.

FLYNN: You can bring Keller out anytime. That kid is smart.

DANE: Why am I not surprised that the two of you hit it off?

FLYNN: What does that mean?

JACK: I think it's a two birds of a feather comment.

FLYNN: For me and Keller? I'll take it.

ME: He's an amazing kid. I'll be proud to call him my son.

ROMEO: You doing that legally or just claiming him with your words?

ME: Legally. Blake is working on the petition of adoption now.

DANE: That's great. Congrats.

ROMEO: Where's the kid?

JACK: Yeah, he normally lives for these group chats.

DANE: Evan! WTF are you?

EVAN: I'm here. Sorry. What did I miss?

FLYNN: What are we missing?

EVAN: What?

ROMEO: Yeah, what's going on with you, Kid? You've been in a shit mood for days.

EVAN: It's that fucking vet bossing me around like I don't know what the hell I'm doing. I was a special forces medic for fuck's sake. I think I can handle a few canine vaccinations.

DANE: Uh-oh.

ROMEO: You are so screwed, my brother.

FLYNN: <gif of cupid shooting off an arrow>

EVAN: I hope you're not suggesting that I'm into her.

BEAU: We would never.

EVAN: Seriously, she's not even nice to me.

EVAN: I don't think she's ever even pretended to smile at me.

EVAN: It doesn't make sense. People always like me.

EVAN: I mean really, have y'all ever met a grumpy veterinarian?

JACK: Well, they do have to deal with some tough situations.

BEAU: Exactly. They lose patients too.

EVAN: I wasn't talking about that.

EVAN: She essentially gets to cuddle dogs and cats all day. Aside from the hard parts, that shit should make you smile.

ROMEO: Haven't seen you smiling around all the dogs.

FLYNN: He's not wrong.

ME: You've been in a bad mood, kid. If you can't deal with the lady doctor, we can transfer that role to someone else.

ME: Romeo could do it.

ROMEO: Romeo is busy trying to get the piece of shit second-hand van we bought up and running.

ME: Minor details.

EVAN: I can work with her.

EVAN: I am a professional

EVAN: She's the grumpy mean one.

epilogue

LIAM

Nine months later...

I hate wearing ties.

Always have. But there are times when I have worn them. Anytime wearing our "dress blues" uniform when I was in active service. My dad's funeral. And my wedding to Wren.

Then there's today.

Wren tells me that it's just a formality, that for intents and purposes, I've been in this role officially for nine months.

Today, I officially become Keller's dad.

On paper. Legally.

About a month after Wren and I married, the Bishops dropped their custody case. Once it became clear to them that no amount of threats would change what had happened. Wren and Keller were safe.

I'm not sure if they'll ever be the kinds of grandparents Keller deserves, but he has so many people in his life that love him, it hardly matters.

He often comes with me to the dog sanctuary. He's a pro now dealing with many of the dogs. He still doesn't want to go into the pen with the pack, but I can't blame him for that. Some of those dogs have nearly knocked me down.

Currently we're standing outside the courtroom where we'll go through the official adoption process.

My wife grabs my hand, drawing my attention to her. She looks gorgeous as usual even though she's been teary-eyed most of this week. Her amber gaze locks with mine.

"I love you," I tell her.

She gives me the sweetest smile. "I know you do. I feel it all the time. I love you."

Keller is sitting on a bench against the wall reading on his new e-reader. He's currently devouring some very long series about cats that talk and are soldiers. I get very lost when he talks about the books mostly because the cats have weird names. In any case, he loves the series and could probably write a dissertation on all of the lore and symbolism throughout.

The heavy wooden door opens and a woman with a clipboard steps outside. "Gardner family." She looks at us questioningly.

"That's us," I say.

"We're ready for you now."

"Keller," Wren says. She holds her hand out to him and he takes it, closing the case on his reader.

The judge sits on an elevated platform, wearing a traditional black robe.

"Good morning," he says.

"Technically it's good afternoon," Keller says. "Because it's nearly twelve thirty."

The judge's eyebrows shoot up. He turns and checks the clock on the way. "Well, right you are, my boy. Thank you for correcting me."

"You're welcome," Keller says.

The judge doesn't even bother to hide his smile. "You must be Keller?"

"Yes."

"Do you know why we're here today?"

"To sign papers so that I can officially call Liam dad."

My throat clogs with his words. This kid.

Wren squeezes my hand.

"Is that something that you want to happen, Keller? You want Liam to be your father?"

"He already is my father. I just want to be able to call him dad," Keller says.

That seems to choke up the judge because he clears his throat a few times, then turns his gaze to me. "That's quite a boy you have there."

"Yes, your honor." I don't dare try to say more because I'd rather not cry all over the courtroom.

"I presume it is your wish to be Keller's father?"

"Yes," I say. "Being this boy's father will be the greatest honor of my life."

"And you must be mom, Wren, is it?"

"Yes, your honor. Do you agree with this petition of adoption?"

"Absolutely."

"Well, then, all of your paperwork is in order. So I don't see a reason to delay this any further." He leans over a sheet of paper and signs it, then hands it to the clerk. "Congratulations, Keller, you've got yourself a dad."

I swallow the lump in my throat, then swipe at my eyes.

"But wait," Keller says.

"What's the matter?" Wren asks.

"He didn't bang his hammer on the desk," Keller says.

"Ah, my gavel," the judge holds up the object of discussion.

"You're supposed to bang that when the case is closed," Kelly explains.

The judge smiles. "Right you are. I think he might be ready for the Supreme Court in a few more years." Then he bangs his gavel.

Keller grabs my hand. "Come on, Dad. Mom said we get ice cream today."

***

I hope you loved Liam and Wren's story. Please consider **leaving me a review**. Want a little more of this sweet couple? Check out the **Bonus Epilogue**.

And YES, of course Winnie is getting her own book. **Big Trouble** will be out soon!

Pre-order the next Dog Tags book, coming next month. **Happily Evan After**

Read the other books in the Dog Tags seres:

Jack of Hearts
Fools Rush Flynn
Quid Pro Beau

Grab **Redeem My Heart** if you want to see where Great Dane's Dog Sanctuary started.

Keep scrolling for an excerpt from another single parent romance, **Short-Term Shag**.

2nd epilogue

WREN

"How're you holding up, Dad?" I ask Liam.

He rolls his eyes, then lays down on his side of the bed. "I'm okay. Didn't know I'd be such a fucking crybaby today though. But I suppose this is why you see family's celebrating Adoption Day. It's not a small thing."

I snuggle up to his bare chest, loving the feel of him. The familiarity of his smell. The way my chin seems to fit just perfectly in the divot under his collarbone. He is my safe place. My happy place.

"No, it's not a small thing at all. Commitment and love, they're choices more than anything. When Keller was a toddler and he wasn't speaking yet, everything was so stressful. Of course, the Bishops and Colt complicated everything. Those years were the hardest of my life because I wanted so desperately to communicate with my son, to know he understood my words.

"I would never have given up on him, but I desperately wanted him to be 'normal.' I hate even saying that. But the way some people spoke to him or about him made me want to claw their eyes out. I thought I wanted things to be easier for him, but the truth was, all of that was about me.

"Me wanting something in my life to be easy or go the way it was supposed to go. Some days I had to fight through the frustration of it all and choose to keep going, keep taking him to Occupational Therapy, keep loving him just the way he was."

"You've done such an amazing job with him," Liam says. "You're so goddamn strong, Songbird. I wish you could see yourself the way I do. But surely you can look at your son and see that he is legit the coolest kid in the world and know that you did that. Your patience and love and commitment. That's why Keller is the way he is."

"Can you believe he corrected the judge?" I ask.

"Twice!"

We both laugh.

"You have no idea how it feels to me to watch you love my son," I tell him. "Thank you for loving him."

"Loving him is the second easiest thing I've ever done."

"What is the first?"

"Loving you."

"Think you'll find room to love more kids someday?" I ask.

"Hell yeah."

"Well, that's a relief. Because I'm pregnant." I drop the bomb and search my husband's face for his reaction.

"I knocked you up?" he asks.

When I nod, he smiles so big that it makes my heart jump. He shifts our positions so I'm laying flat on the bed. Then he crawls down to my belly, the one that hasn't been flat since high school. The one with stretch marks and a cesarian section scar. And I feel not one bit of apprehension or discomfort.

Because I know that this man loves me. He shows me that every day.

He pulls up my sleep shirt and lays his head on my belly. "Hello in there. This is your daddy." Liam looks up at me, wonder etched in his features. "I don't know when they can start hearing."

"We have a ways to go before that happens, but nothing wrong with talking to them anyways. I did it with Keller my entire pregnancy."

"I didn't think you could get any sexier," he says, his voice taking that dark and rich tone.

I raise my eyebrows at him.

"It's true, Wren. I'm going to enjoy watching your body change while you grow our baby. I love you so fucking much."

"I love you. I'm so glad you're happy about the baby."

"And Keller calls me 'dad' now. Almost the best fucking day of my life."

"What's the best?"

"When you finally became my wife."

"This feels like how my life was supposed to

be. I know that everything we both went through to get here made us who we are today and I wouldn't want to change that. But everything with you feels so right," I tell him.

"Damn fucking straight." He moves again, this time lying on his back. "Now, get up on here and sit on my face, wife. I am craving your sweet pussy."

"Again? Didn't we do this last night?"

"You complaining?" he asks.

I laugh. "Of course not."

He pats his chest. "Then climb up here, my queen."

I quickly stand, stripping off my sleep shorts and my shirt. His dark eyes grow even darker while he watches me. His hand goes to his enormous erection, barely contained by his boxers. He grips it tight.

I crawl up the bed rubbing my tits over his dick.

"Fuck me, you're so sexy, wife."

I keep going up his torso, but then in a move that surprises both of us, I turn so I'm facing his dick. My needy core hovers over his face.

"Yes," he hisses. He wraps his arms around my thighs and pulls me down to him.

The first swipe of his tongue makes me moan. He's so damn good at that. I try to concentrate on what I'm doing before he makes me lose my mind.

I pull out his cock, it's heavy and hot against my palm. I don't bother with any big seduction, just leave down and suck him into my mouth.

"Christ, Wren," he growls against my tender flesh. Then he licks and sucks relentlessly until I'm rocking against his face.

I do my best to stay focused on what I'm doing to his cock, but it's so hard when he's got me riding the line between pleasure and bliss.

He swats my ass to let me know he's there and I swallow him down as he pours into my throat. Then I'm coming too. Riding his tongue until I nearly see stars.

I collapse on the bed next to him. "Holy shit," I breathe.

"Yeah. Give me twenty minutes and we can do that again."

I laugh. "Insatiable."

"For you? Always."

***

I hope you loved Liam and Wren's story. Please consider **leaving me a review**.

And YES, of course Winnie is getting her own book. **Big Trouble**, keep scrolling for an excerpt!

Read the other books in the Dog Tags series:

Jack of Hearts
Fools Rush Flynn
Quid Pro Beau
Love 'em or Liam
Happily Evan After
Ready, Willing and Abel
Romero and Juliette

Grab **Redeem My Heart** if you want to see where Great Dane's Dog Sanctuary started.

thank you for reading!

Join my newsletter for bonus epilogues, deleted scenes and a FREE BOOK.

join me!

COME JOIN my **VIP Reader Group on Facebook** where I do sneak peeks, answer questions and keep you up to date with everyone going on in Kat Baxter land.

excerpt from big trouble

Official Rules for *Wind from the East Nanny Service*

Rule #1: Nannies shall maintain their composure at all times, even when dealing with difficult topics.

Winnie's take away: Do not talk about penises when talking to your hot boss. Moreover, do not think about his penis while talking about penises.

WINNIE

I've been fired from a lot of jobs. Too many, in truth. I can't say that none of them have been justified. I did actually catch the Murphy's kitchen on fire while dog sitting. But it's not my fault that the homemade dog treat recipe was so flammable or that their smoke detectors were so sensitive. The fire was contained entirely to their oven, and there was (almost) no damage. In my defense, I'd been seventeen at the time. You get what you pay for.

But a lot of the dismissals have been due to circumstances out of my control. A power outage flipped a switch, and I didn't know to check the breaker on the ice cream freezer. Yeah, that had been a huge mess. I'd not only been fired, but strongly encouraged to not even return to Rosie's Diner as a customer.

As for the job at the pet store ... well, they never told me I couldn't bring home the dying Beta fish and rehabilitate them. The "company policy" of flushing them down the toilet seemed both cruel and environmentally irresponsible. And it's not like I was going to sell the fish myself once I got them healthy. I had planned to bring them back! Honestly, I think Dale, the assistant manager, just used the Beta fish scandal as an excuse to fire me since I'd turned him down for coffee four times in a row.

Even if I had wanted to date a man twelve years older than me with halitosis, everyone knows you don't date your boss!

But this scenario?

This current scenario is new for me.

For starters, I need this job. Like, *need* need this job. Like, I will be living out of my car if I lose this job. And since "my car" is a rusted-out Ford Focus that's older than I am, that is not an option.

Secondly, this is a job that I actually care

about and that I'm qualified to do. Over-qualified, if I do say so myself, since I have a degree in childhood development.

Thirdly, in the two hours since I've first showed up, everything has gone perfectly. I was greeted at the door by Mrs. Billingsly, the cook/housekeeper, who was immediately friendly and gracious. I met the dog, some kind of hyperactive doodle mix named Banana-Noodle, who slobbered all over me and rolled over to show her belly. The obviously grumpy cat named SnickerDoodle only growled at me once. And then there's Clementine.

Insert blissful sigh here...

Clementine Callahan, aka the girl I'm here to nanny for, is an adorable seven-year-old, with bouncy red curls, a sassy mouth, and more energy than... well, a hyperactive doodle mix.

She's clearly too smart for her own good, and a trouble maker, and I am here for it.

Clementine has already given me a tour of the house, a sprawling, oversized ranch house that's obviously been recently upgraded. The furniture is as oversized as the rooms, and the views of the horse ranch and the surrounding mountains are simply spectacular. I've seen the pool, the barn, and the chicken coop.

Hell, Clementine has already painted my toes and braided my hair. Only on one side before getting distracted, but still, I get it.

She wanted to show off her reading skills. A girl who would rather read than style hair is a girl after my own heart.

So there we were, me, Clementine, and Banana-Noodle, sitting on a mound of pillows by the window in the playroom, reading one of my favorite books, Mercy Watson Fights Crime–because, of course, Clementine has excellent taste in books–when *he* comes in.

He is Brody Callahan, Clementine's father, and my new boss.

He takes one stony-eyed look at me before growling that he needs to see me in his office.

The moment my gaze meets his, I know what's coming. He's going to fire me. I've been through this enough that I recognize the signs.

Despite my employment record, I haven't had time to screw anything up. I've been at work for less than two hours.

Nevertheless, I follow him down the hall to a

home office filled with bulky furniture and leather seating. Clearly a man's room.

He throws his oversized body into an over-sized chair and glares at me some more before standing up and pacing.

When he still doesn't say anything, I go on the offensive. "I have excellent qualifications," I blurt.

"I was expecting a man," the huge man says, before I can list them.

"Oookay," I draw out the word, putting together the pieces of this rapidly unfolding puzzle. "I might have picked up on that subtle undercurrent of testosterone-fueled disap-pointment."

"I thought—"

"That I had a penis?" I don't give him a chance to respond before I add, "I'd say I get that a lot, but honestly, this has never happened before."

"What kind of woman is named Winslow?" the man growls.

I stare at his angry, glowering, and yet still stupidly handsome face.

"You'd have to ask my parents. I'm told it's

because they'd been assured I was a boy and had already settled on the name," I explain.

He just stares at me as if the words I've said are gibberish. "I hired a male nanny."

"You *thought* you hired a male nanny. As you can tell, I am very much a woman."

His gaze drops as he takes in my generous curves.

He growls, and I'm a little worried about that vein that's bulging on his forehead.

"You cannot actually fire me for not being a man. That's sexism, which I'm sure you realize is illegal," I say.

"This is not a corporation we're talking about. This is my home and my daughter."

"Yes. You have a lovely home. Your adorable and, might I add, very smart daughter gave me a tour earlier."

He jabs a finger at his own chest. "I get to decide who lives here and takes care of her."

"Of course you do. You just cannot fire me based on the fact that I have a vagina rather than a penis. I already signed a contract. Are there some sort of tasks that require the Y-chromosome?"

I stare at the hulking man in front of me.

He's practically vibrating with anger, yet I feel zero fear being in his presence. Even though I'm sure much of that anger is directed at me, he doesn't make me feel unsafe.

He's impossibly tall and broad. The term 'as big as a side of a barn' comes to mind. There's nothing particularly unique about his brown hair. But the brown beard he sports does nothing to hide the fact that his jawline is masculine perfection. Like God carved it by hand on a day when He was feeling particularly generous. And I can tell from the amount of glaring he does, that his jaw muscles are ones he works out on a regular basis.

He's like part cowboy, part mountain man. Wranglers mold to his thighs like they are stretched beyond reason to encompass his thick, thick legs. I'm dying to see what they do for his booty, but I obviously am not going there. Like I said, everyone knows you don't date your boss. Nor should you ogle said boss's tushy.

The black t-shirt is barely containing his massive shoulders and boulder-sized biceps. This man is legit enormous. I wish I could say that his grumpy face made me find him repulsive, but alas, that is not the case.

He's rudely hot.

"This is not going to work," he says with a defiant shake of his head.

Before I can respond, he stomps past me.

He pauses at the office door and snaps, without looking back at me, "I want you gone by the time I get back."

A moment later, I hear the front door slam.

I sink into one of the nearby armchairs. No, no, no, no, no, no.

"I can not lose this job," I mutter, burying my head in my hands, only to sit bolt upright when I see a flash of movement out of the corner of my eye. "Clementine?" I ask. "Is that you?"

A blur of red hair dashes across the room and hits me square in the chest as she throws herself into my arms.

"He can't fire you!" she screeches. "He always fires the nannies, and it's not fair. You didn't buy any animals or accidentally fall asleep in his bed or steal his pickles or anything!"

I wrap my arms around her, patting her back. "Don't worry, Clem. I'm not going anywhere."

I was already prepared to fight for this job, because it's perfect for me, and I need it, and I'm too tall to sleep in my Focus! But now?

Now that Clementine is begging me to stay? Hell yes, I'm keeping this job.

Mr. Grouchy-Pants-Brooding-Brody will have to pry this job out of my cold, dead hands.

She pulls back enough to blink her tear-laden lashes at me. "Promise?"

I hold out my hand, little finger extended. "Even better. I pinkie promise."

She gives me the side-eye. "What's that mean?"

I take her hand in mine and fold in her fingers so that her pinkie is extended, then give her pinkie a shake with my own. "It's a special promise just between girls that says I'm not leaving, I'm not quitting, and I'm definitely not ..." I trail off, racking my brain for a third thing before latching on to what Clementine said earlier. "... going to steal your father's pickles."

I'm still thinking about that an hour later, when Mr. Broody-Brody still hasn't returned, and I'm unpacking my things in the guest quarters that are located directly above the master suite of the house. Mrs. Billingsly assured me that this is where I'll be staying. And I've even gotten a text from the lawyer who sent the original paperwork, assuring me that I am not fired.

What exactly did all those other nannies do to get fired? Sure, buying pets without a parent's permission is clearly problematic.

With a man that looks like that? I'm sure that's how one of the nannies "accidentally" fell asleep in his bed.

But stealing his pickles? What is that about?

Not that it's any of my business.

I just need to do my job. Focus on Clementine. Keep my head down and my hands off his pickles. Whatever the hell that means.

Grab your copy of **Big Trouble**

about the author

USA Today Bestselling Author, Kat Baxter writes fast-paced, sweet & STEAMY romantic comedies. Readers have dubbed her "The Queen of Adorkable." and her books "laugh-out-loud funny," and "hot enough to melt your kindle." She lives in Texas with her family and a menagerie of animals. Kat is the pseudonym for a bestselling historical romance author.

What readers have said about Kat's books:

"Kat Baxter is my catnip!" ~ Goodreads review

"Whenever I need my sexy nerdy dirty talking romance fix, I know Kat Baxter has my back!" ~Goodreads review

"How does Kat Baxter make me fall in love with her characters in just 12 short chapters? It's coz she's a freaken magic weaver with her words!!" ~ Amazon review

"You'll instantly fall in love." ~Goodreads review

"Swoon. I could not get enough of this story and fell in love with both these characters!" ~Amazon review

"... the chemistry between them is instant and off the charts!" ~Amazon review

"... original, hot, and a hoot!" ~Amazon review

"DAMN it's hot." ~Amazon review

"... sweetness, heat and humor. By the time the story was over, my cheeks hurt from smiling so hard." ~Amazon review

"Such a very sweet and spicy story!" ~ Goodreads

"The connection between the characters felt real, and I liked the author's writing style." ~ Goodreads

Made in the USA
Coppell, TX
20 January 2026